For bear lovers everywhere
M.W.

For Helen Margaret, with love
M.C.

First published by
Walker Books Ltd,
87 Vauxhall Walk, London SE11 5HJ

First published 1996

Text © 1996 Martin Waddell
Illustrations © 1996 Margaret Chamberlain

2 4 6 8 10 9 7 5 3 1

This book has been typeset in Century Old Style.

Printed in Great Britain

ISBN 0-7445-5101-3

BEARS EVERYWHERE

MARTIN WADDELL
MARGARET CHAMBERLAIN

WALKER BOOKS
AND SUBSIDIARIES
LONDON • BOSTON • SYDNEY

Alice liked bears, so she put up a sign
on her house.

Along came a bear.
"I'm a bear from Bear Wood," said the bear.
"Will I do?"
"Come right in, Bear," replied Alice.

Alice played games
with her bear.

Bear-hug …

and Bear-chase …

and Bear-hide-and-seek.

"More! More! More!
More!" shouted Alice.
"Then you need more bears!"
panted Alice's bear, and he
sent out for more to Bear Wood.

Three little bears came in from Bear Wood,
and the three little bears played with Alice.

"More! More! More! More!" shouted Alice.
So Alice's bear sent for more bears from
Bear Wood. They were hip-swinging,
ring-a-ding bears!

One really cool bear played the piano and
sang, and some of them danced on the porch.

They took turns at dancing
with Alice, till Alice was puffed.

"More! More! More! More!" shouted Alice,
and more and more bears came out of
Bear Wood.

They went swimming with Alice
down at the creek.

The moon rose over Bear Wood as Alice
came sleepily home from the creek.

When Alice got back to her house,
the bear party was still going on.

There were bears
in the cupboards
and bears on
the stairs.

Bears looking
at pictures
and climbing
on chairs.

There were bears everywhere!

Four bears were tucked up in Alice's bed,
and the four bears were snoring.

"There are bears in
my bed so I'll sleep in the
bath," Alice said, grabbing
a blanket off one of the bears, but …

There was a bear
in the bath
playing boats.

Two bears were queueing to
get in the shower. Three bears
were looking for towels.

A small bear was using the toothpaste to write SMALL BEAR WAS HERE on the mirror.

And the smallest of all of the bears was curled up asleep in the basin.

"There are too many bears now!" Alice cried.
"I thought there might be," said Alice's bear. And Alice's bear shouted, "Bears out!" Out rushed the bears. Bears climbed through the windows. Bears shot out through the doors.

Bears squeezed up the chimney. Bears popped out from under the floors. There were bears everywhere, running off into Bear Wood!

"Now you've only one bear left," said Alice's bear.
"*One* bear's just what I wanted," said Alice.
And …

Alice's bear stayed with Alice.